RANDOM KAK

I Remember about growing up in South Africa

Trevor Romain

PENGUIN BOOKS

PENGUIN BOOKS

Published by the Penguin Group
Penguin Books (South Africa) (Pty) Ltd, Registered Office: Block D, Rosebank Office Park, 181 Jan Smuts Avenue,
Parktown North, Johannesburg, 2193, South Africa

www.penguinbooks.co.za

First published by Penguin Books South Africa 2013

Copyright © Trevor Romain 2013

ISBN 978-0-14-353817-2
eISBN 978-0-14-353108-1

Printed and bound by CTP Printers, Cape Town

The author and publishers are grateful for permissions granted to reproduce commercial brands in this publication.
While every effort has been made to trace all brand owners, we would invite any left out to get in touch with us so
that we could rectify any omission. The Jackie logo is used with kind permission of DC Thomson & Co. Ltd.

For my mother Carmel,
my boet Steve and my sister Elise.
In memory of my late dad Jac Romain.

I was delivered at the
Frangwyn Nursing
Home in Jo'burg.
I was born at a
very young age so
I don't remember
much about it. But
I do remember a lot
of other random kak about
growing up in South Africa...

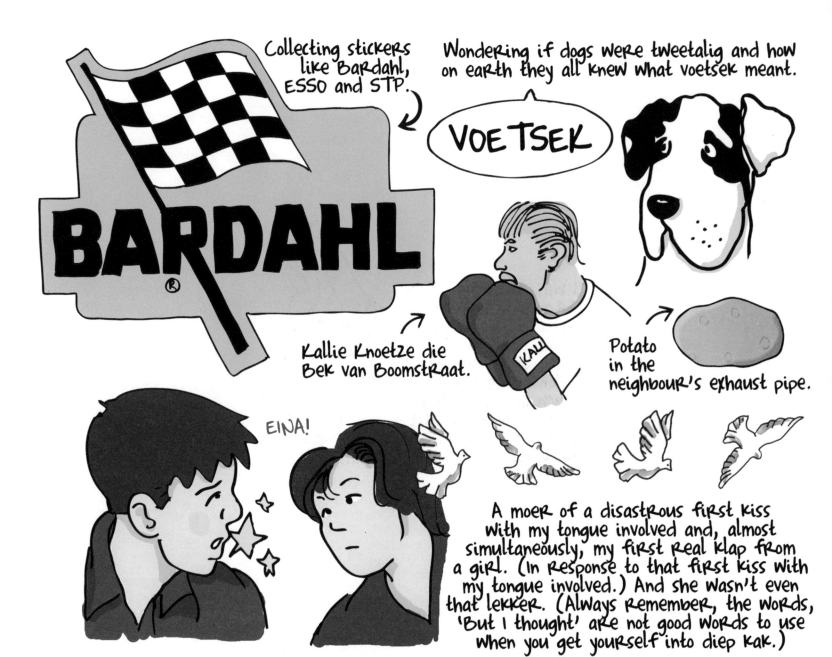

Collecting stickers like Bardahl, ESSO and STP.

Wondering if dogs were tweetalig and how on earth they all knew what voetsek meant.

VOETSEK

BARDAHL®

Kallie Knoetze die Bek van Boomstraat.

Potato in the neighbour's exhaust pipe.

EINA!

A moer of a disastrous first kiss with my tongue involved and, almost simultaneously, my first real klap from a girl. (In response to that first kiss with my tongue involved.) And she wasn't even that lekker. (Always remember, the words, 'But I thought' are not good words to use when you get yourself into diep kak.)

2

Failing standard six.
What a skaam.

Hubbly Bubbly cold drink made in Jo'burg.

Before a matinee at the local bioscope the American guys from Coke, with their very serious red jackets, would give yo-yo demonstrations. Then I tried it out when I got to my grandparents' farm for a weekend. I gooied a 'round the world' and the string came off my finger and I almost bloody moered my granny on the head with the yo-yo.

Patching the inner tube for my ten speed with a patch kit.

TUBE
PATCH
KIT

DO NOT USE ON CUTS.

The bottle had little dents to look like bubbles.

Coca-Cola

Watching 'The World At War' on TV.

3

STP stickers made a car go faster!

My first movie star crush. Tracy Hyde who played Melody. It was so pitiful. I even wrote her a love letter. And believe it or not...she didn't write back. I was heartbroken. She bust up with me before we even started dating. Damn.

My mom spending hours and hours sewing little printed name tags into my school uniform. (Mind you it was a green safari suit with a school badge if you remember.)

As a laaitie how upset I was when the horse 'Sea Cottage' was shot three weeks before the Durban July but survived and still ran the race.

Short back and sides haircuts.

My dad hammering planks onto the tree in the garden so we could climb up the trunk and get into the branches.

Rubbing Wintergreen on your legs before a Rugby game.

WINTERGREEN

Rubbing Wintergreen too close to your nuts before a Rugby game!

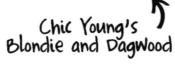
Chic Young's Blondie and Dagwood

Having to put on a tie for school every friggin' morning!

Just about kakking myself upon hearing that our new PT instructor in the army's name was Vleis.

Making a blowtorch with a match and a can of hairspray.

Blackjacks.

Jane Seymour

Wonderset hairspray

Popping blue bottles with a stick or your flip-flops at the beach.

Slap chips and oily Russian or Vienna sausages.

16 mm movies.

EIKI

Spending bloody hours wrapping school books in brown paper and plastic on the first day of school!

trevor

7

South African Railways.
Suid-Afrikaanse Spoorweg. The good old
milk train to Cape town. Half asleep, quietly comfortable,
under the clean white sheets, on my cabin bunk-bed as the train gently
Rocked while winding its way through the Karoo in the middle of the night.

Feeling really bad for Zola Budd when she collided with Mary Decker at the olympics. Thinking, even though she was in a stadium full of people, how lonely she must have felt.

Youth Preparedness or cadets at school. Where shell-shocked old teachers re-lived their war years.

Nix

The book that made me want to be a WRITER.

Keith and Lorna Stevens'

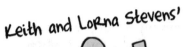

flip foster

Under my bed, in the still of the night, the sound of silkworms eating mulberry leaves in an old shoe box with holes punched through the lid with a ballpoint pen.

Put a tiger in your tank.

Klaring out of the army!

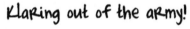

When I was a little oke and I pulled faces my ma warned me that, if the wind changed, I would stay like that forever. (And I friggin' believed her. I still lick my finger and hold it up to the wind before I make a face.)

Being pulled behind a bicycle on a skateboard and then trying to take a corner. I still have the scars to prove it.

Playing cricket with a wooden fruit crate for wickets.

My gran always had Quality Street toffees for us when we went to visit.

Go school.

Go school.

Doing the school war cry during a rugby game and being so proud.

Great milkshakes from the Milky Lane.

Leaving empty milk bottles outside with green plastic discs in them and hearing the milkman, clinking bottles, through early morning sleep, when he delivered fresh milk at dawn almost every day.

Harvest
Neil Young

My favourite making-out music when I was a teenager.

Queen at Sun City. That was the best joll ever!

Old ballies leaning to the side while playing bowls in their white outfits. (I remember wondering if leaning would really help the ball curve towards the kitty.)

Chorb Cream

Matric dance ↗

My matric dance. Ag it was lekker man. Except for the green suit I wore. Nooit. What was I thinking?

The movie Jaws.

This often happened to the number ten bus at Gallagher's Corner in Orange Grove. ↘

The long pole the bus conductors used to put the connecting rod from the bus back on the electric overhead line when it came off if the driver took a corner too sharply. →

'Get big bubble fun with chappies bubblegum, gives you flavour by the ton, lots of colours to choose from. Everybody knows the one. Chappies bubble gum.'

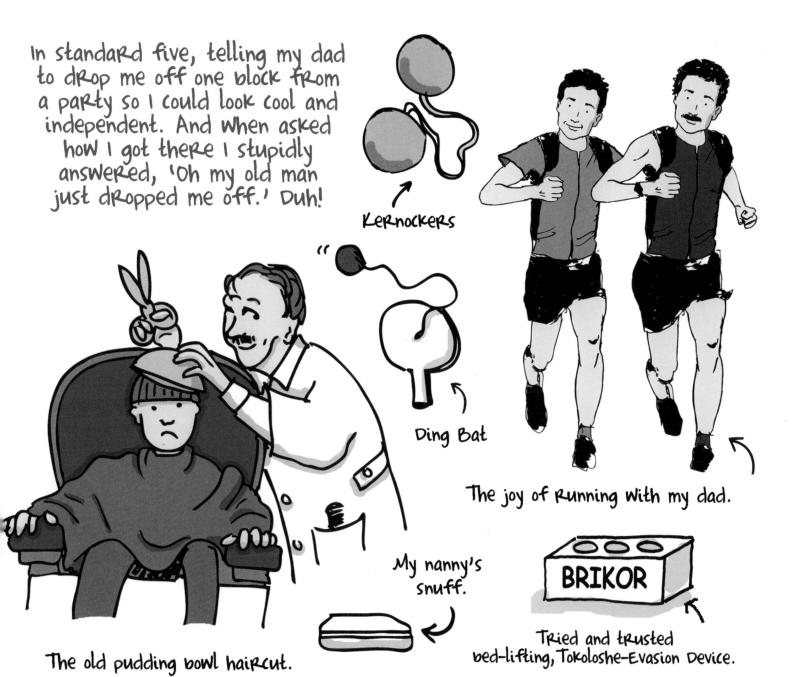

In standard five, telling my dad to drop me off one block from a party so I could look cool and independent. And when asked how I got there I stupidly answered, 'Oh my old man just dropped me off.' Duh!

Kernockers

Ding Bat

The joy of running with my dad.

The old pudding bowl haircut.

My nanny's snuff.

BRIKOR

Tried and trusted bed-lifting, Tokoloshe-Evasion Device.

Mampoer hurts!

Down a lion. Feel satisfied.

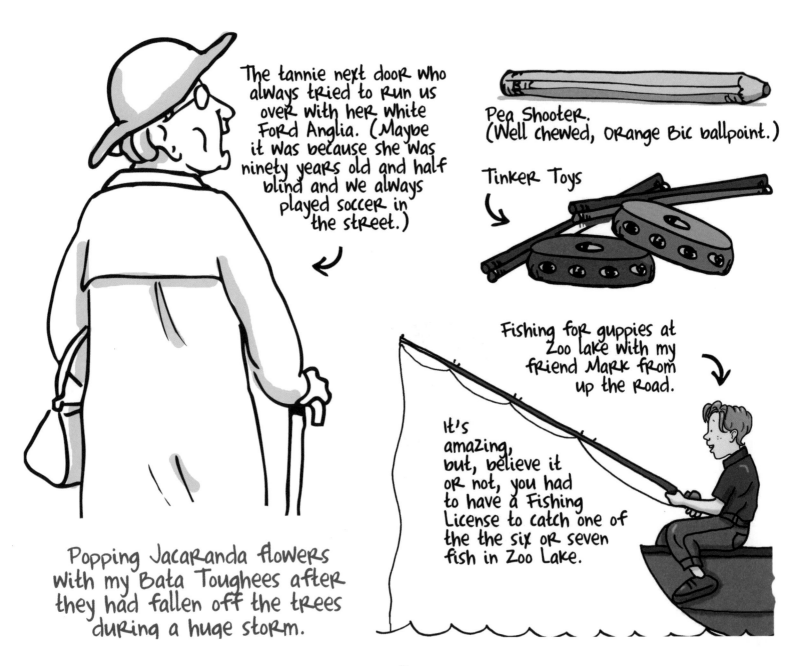

The tannie next door who always tried to run us over with her white Ford Anglia. (Maybe it was because she was ninety years old and half blind and we always played soccer in the street.)

Pea Shooter.
(Well chewed, orange Bic ballpoint.)

Tinker Toys

Fishing for guppies at Zoo Lake with my friend Mark from up the road.

It's amazing, but, believe it or not, you had to have a Fishing License to catch one of the the six or seven fish in Zoo Lake.

Popping Jacaranda flowers with my Bata Toughees after they had fallen off the trees during a huge storm.

Listening to my favourite DJs Stan Katz (whom I worked for once) John Berks and the fantastic Cocky Two-Bull Thotlhalemaje (The first black DJ) on Channel 702.

A memorial to my teens. The Radium Beer hall. Birthplace of my delinquency.

I loved photography at high school. Everyone told me I was crazy to go into the Sebokeng Location to take pictures. Contrary to popular belief, people there welcomed me and loved being photographed especially the kids. A few eyebrows were raised when I won first prize at school for a picture of a giggling girl, in the township, all dressed with a vaseline sheen and a room-warming, radiant smile.

The Wits Rag. With students dressed in animal costumes and fancy dress clothes on floats. And drommies. Yes drommies in lekker pom-pom outfits. It was fun. And the Wits-Wits magazine.

Coming short off a drain pipe while climbing up to a chick's bedroom window one floor above and falling into the flowerbed as the rusty pipe collapsed. The things we did for love. Like walking in the rain and the snow when there's nowhere to go, etc.

The first time I saw my little bro Steve!

My sar'nt Major's mouth!

'Tree aan julle naaiers! Staaldak. Webbing. En geweer. Julle troepies gaan nou 'n bietjie kots.'

S.A. WEERMAG—S.A. DEFENCE FORCE

Dear Mr Romain,
JY GAAN KAAK!

Report to Milner Park Station and leave your ma at home. Sy gaan huil.

First teen heartbreak. Jirre that was kak hey.
I even remember a song that played over and over in
my mind. 'Raindrops Keep Falling On My Head'.

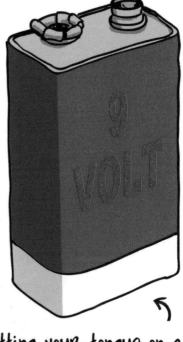

Putting your tongue on a 9 volt
battery. (Don't ask because
I don't know the answer.)

The beautiful stillness of an old station while
driving through the Karoo in the early
morning on the way to Cape Town. And the
breathtaking sight of Namaqualand Daisies as
they opened up to follow the sun across the sky.

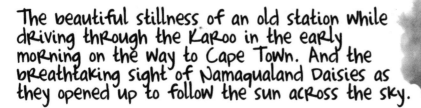

My first car. A Mini van den Plas. (And yes, that is a skaam basket-weave pattern on the side. And no, I don't know why. I'd love to go back in time and ask myself the same question.)

'It's not inside...it's on top.'

the word Schloep

Putting a mirror on my shoe at school and trying to look up Mrs Lombard's dress.

Being wrapped in a warm towel after swimming in the sea.

Getting a klap upside my head for putting a mirror on my shoe at school and trying to look up Mrs Lombard's dress.

Vaccinations at school.

Having a cup of tea with my ma after my grandpa died.

Listening to LM Radio. 'Aqui Portugal Mocambique, fala-vos Radio Clube em Lourenco Marques transmintindo em ondas curtas e medias.'

I was always totally poep scared of marionettes and some puppets especially those Punch and Judy characters who totally freaked the hell out of me.

But on the other hand I loved the cuddly Raggedy Anne and Andy my sweet mom made for me.

Making go-carts using pram wheels and then getting into kak for stealing the wheels off your sister's buggered up old pram to do so. Even though the pram sat in the back yard for years just in case another kid came along.

TEACHER'S
HIGHLAND CREAM
W
BLENDED
SCOTCH WHISKY

My boet filled up a bottle of scotch that my dad had with tea water that looked exactly like the scotch. My dad didn't drink scotch but discovered the switch a few years later when he poured his buddy a drink.

Wanting to be a biplane pilot and war ace after visiting the war museum next door to the zoo in Jo'burg as a young lightie.

Jumping off the Roof into a swimming pool.

We played marbles every day. We collected the marbles in bank bags including ironies, puries and ghoens. And we used phrases like nicky bomb drops and shy here a four man. (Marbles also worked very well as katty ammuntion.)

Ghoen

Stove Pipes

My art teacher Mr Louw, who said I wasn't talented enough to take art for Matric. (Se moer.)

Lagging our gats off when a polisieman came short and fell on his pip while chasing a local gardener down the street because he didn't have a pass book. Much to our delight (and cheering) the gardener got away. The copper got up and was so the moer in with us, because we laughed at his sorry arse, that he chased after us. But we all ducked in different directions and the cop got back into his yellow van and buggered off. The gardener was back an hour later chipper as ever and continued mowing the pavement lawn.

After listening to my dad's advice and not taking any crap from anyone, I about kakked a brick when I told the oke who always bullied me to, 'Bugger off. Stop tuning me grief and take a pill and dissolve.' (So much for standing up for yourself. The ou got woes, just about had a thrombosis, and gave me a moer of a lamer.)

First beer at the Radium after school (with school blazer stashed in my haversack.)

Warming school clothes over the heater on a winter morning.

Trompie en die Boksombende met Rooie, Blikkies, Dawie en Boesman die brak.

MOEILIKHEID

There is no translation for the phrase, 'You are stripping my moer, bliksem.'

How we listened to the moon landing on the radio while the rest of the world watched it on TV. Even in Rhodesia.

Carving on a desk and even spelling my own name wrong! →

How we would quickly scramble to touch our heads, and then touch our feet and say, 'Touch my head, touch my toes, never to go in one of those,' when an ambulance came past.

The brekers smoking and making kak at the back of the bus upstairs. If you turned and looked you could expect a nice klap upside the back of your head followed by some raucous laughter.

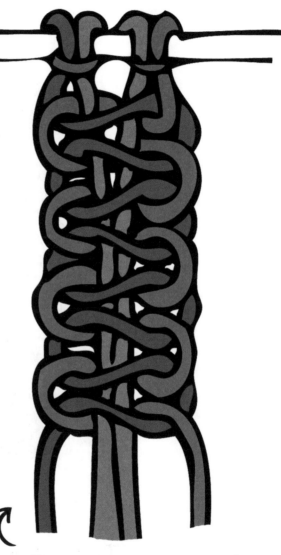

Making scoubidous at school.

35

The classic poster I had in my bedroom.

Patrick Mynhardt
as Herman Charles
Bosman's Oom
Schalk Lourens.
The oke was classic.

Realising the serious-looking municipal official, who took me for my driving test, had no sense of humour when I asked him if he was scared.

Watching the movie 'Love Story' with some ous and trying my best not to cry, but a tear sneaked out. You should have checked how fast I wiped it away hey.

Shooting sky rockets out of coke bottles at each other. Idiots!

Feeling sorry for Wolraad Woltemade's horse.

Pulling a loose tooth out of my head by tying a string to the door and slamming it shut.

Calling a fight a rought.

Using a rotary phone where you actually 'dialed' someone's number.

Frustrated that I couldn't be a hippy because we were not allowed to have long hair at our school.

Doing a bollemakiesie.

The dog across the road was demented and definitely a shizoid. Some days she was a sweetie and other days she'd hide behind a wall, sneak up and sink her teeth into the back of your unsuspecting leg. I swear I heard her chuckle when she ran away, unless it was just her clearing shredded denim from her throat.

'Romain. How come every time I see you I just wanna #$@ klap you?' - Col Hugo

I was heartbroken when my first girlfriend (the love of my life) left South Africa when I was in Standard six to live overseas. The big problem was... she had no clue that we were going steady. Actually, to tell the truth, I don't think she liked me very much at all. Ag shame hey.

Using a pencil to wind a cassette tape.

Enid Blyton's Noddy and Big Ears.

Collecting bullet-heads from the Huddle Park Gun Range and melting them in a pot over a fire. And breaking open thermometers to play with the mercury. No wonder I'm dyslexic. Mercury and Lead are not good for children and other living things.

Vat hom Dawie
9

Dawie de Villiers

The Radio show 'Taxi' with Chuck Edwards, old Red Kowolski and Chuck's chick Myrtle in New York city. 'If I don't see you through the week. I'll see you through the window.'

The movie Rocky

TAXI

Learning how to be a skilled fighting machine during basics
in the army by cleaning a Unimog truck with a toothbrush.

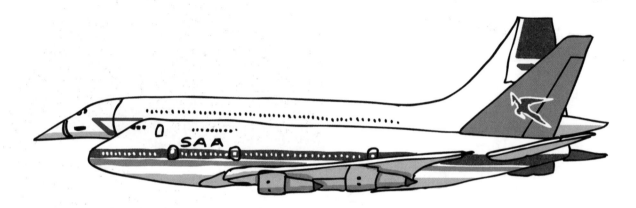

Seeing a Jumbo 747 flying alongside the Concord during break at school.
(The Concord was doing high altitude take off tests at Jan Smuts.)

Calling a swimming pool a goefies or a ghoet pond.

Kreepy Krauly

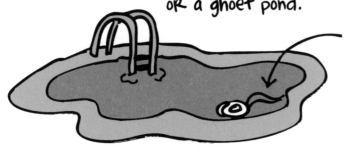

Buying my first transistor radio at Hilton Radio but it was cheap and kak and the only clear radio station I could get was Highveld playing songs by James Last, Gē Korsten and Mimi Coetzer.

While waiting to get cuts from the principal the school secretary saying, 'Mr. Romain. Why am I not surprised to see you again?'

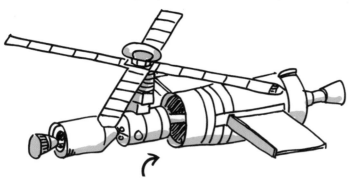

Waiting for Skylab to fall on our house.

George, a sweet Indian guy, who brought great fruit and veggies to our house, on a truck, every week.

VERY FRESH FRUITS AND VEG

Wondering why Parktown Prawns always friggin' made themselves at home in MY shoes. Yuck. Gives me the grils.

Boris Spasky vs Bobby Fischer 1966 chess game. It was broadcast on the radio worldwide.

Having the balls to say, 'I love you' first to a stukkie and getting the old 'I know,' as a response. (How kak is that?)

Being proud of Gerrie Coetzee.

Photo comics which some parents would not allow their kids to read.

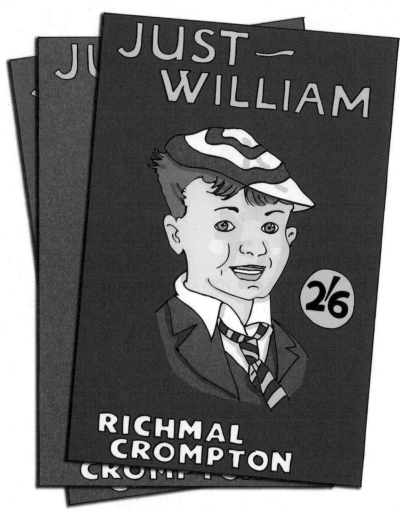

Books my dad read to me.

Watching an inept cop trying to shoot an escaped baboon high up in a tree in our neighbourhood. He had one eye squinted closed and his tongue was out as he aimed. He was using his old nineteen-voetsak service revolver, which was attached to a leather holster with a lekker chain. 'Stand back,' he yelled before each shot. He missed totally.

Francoise Hardy

Making a lekker whip from a willow tree.

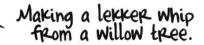

Sharing a sarmie with my dad during break when he lost his job and came to my school for a term to teach Industrial Arts. Shame man, he didn't fit in with the stuffy teachers so he came and sat with me on the stone wall by the rugby fields and we ate lunch. I miss that oke so much.

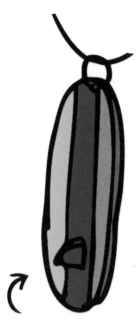

Making a mini
surfboard
necklace with
Perspex.

The smell of Dettol after you scraped
the hell out of yourself as a little
kid. And your mom was dabbing the
wound and you were crying your eyes
out because it stung like hell.

Boo!

Being told that giving someone
a fright would stop hiccups.

Dettol

BRIKOR

BRIKOR

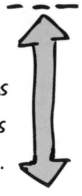

When a
short
person was
called
two bricks
and a
ticky high.

Alan Gold singing
at any steak house including the Turn
and Tender in Highlands North and
Charlie C's in Orange Grove. I never
saw that oke in a bad mood.

Always being intrigued by the McPhail building with it's 'Mac Won't Phail you' slogan. McPhail trucks brought coal to our house in big sacks that were dumped in our back yard.

The Fafi man. A little Chinese guy trying to disguise himself with a big hat while taking money for bets from ousies on the pavement.

"Fah-fee anybodeee?"

Also known as a Lucky Dip

Watching The Gods Must Be Crazy.

Someone said I was so skinny that if I lifted my arms I'd fall through my own arse-hole. That's when those body buidling devices on the back page of comics became a much sought-after item!

Mercurochrome

My first french kiss. (At a social. Remember those?) I didn't realise you were NOT supposed to prod someone's tonsils and gag them with your tongue.

Ag sies man!

Surprising your pal by frantically pumping a bicycle pump and touching the metal part to the back of his neck. This was usually followed by a scream and an eina and a high probability of a punch in your face. (But you still did it.)

Rugby players with great names like Blikkies, Rampie, Lappies and Os.

Trying to catch birds with a box and string.

Using Pritt glue to paste pictures from the panorama magazine for school projects.

Being dragged along on a Saturday morning to the OK Bazaars.

Radio shows including Test The Team, Tracey Dark, Squaddies, The Omo Show 21, The World at 7pm (with Dennis Smith or Victor Mackison reporting), No Place to Hide with Mark Saxon and Sergei, Inspector Carr Investigates, Call Back The Past with Percy Sieff, The Creaking Door, The Top Twenty hosted by Gruesome Gresham, the Chappie Chipmunk Club, Brian O'Shaughnessy as Jet Jungle, Test the Team with Dewar McCormack and Venture with Kim Shippey. Let us not forget, The Surf Show Pick-A-Box with Bob Courtney, the Caltex Show with Peter Merrill, Check Your Mate with Percy Sieff and Judy Henderson and the good old Forces Favourites with Esmé.

Running Red Rover. A game we played but that I damn hated because I always got moered. I was always bloody well first!
'Red Rover, Red Rover let Trevor come over.'
'Aaaaiiieeeee...'

Disco

The song:
'They're coming to take me away ha ha, he he, ho ho, to the funny farm where life is beautiful all the time.'

Almost kakking my rods when we were taken on our roofie ride in those old green Bedford trucks from the Potch station to our first day in the army at 4th field regiment.

Every school had a smoker's corner.

My dad's definition of a hippy: A Jack who looks like a Jill and smells like a John.

Watching the movie 'Woodstock' at least five times at His Majesty's in Johannesburg.

The clean, crisp smell of Sunlight soap.

How proud I felt when I got my first flat in Sandringham, Jo'burg.

The teacher who did such a great job in making me HATE maths!

I remember my dad taking me on a Sunday afternoon outing to Jan Smuts Airport where we would have a toasted cheese and watch the planes from the observation deck outside.

Making Shongololos curl up by touching them with a stick.

BOOM!

Goscinny and Uderzo's Asterix and Obelix.

I was very little and we heard the explosion when the Modderfontein dynamite factory blew up.

Haas Das.

The guilt and awkwardness of seeing my nanny's pass book for the first time.

The original piss cat.

Calling a person Skinny Malinky Long Legs.

'Skinny Malinky Long-Legs
vRot banana feet went to the bioscope
And couldn't find a seat
Sat on a lady...Out popped a baby
Skinny Malinky Long-Legs vRot banana feet'

I was teased a lot as a kid. I sometimes felt like Charlie Brown...

with hair.

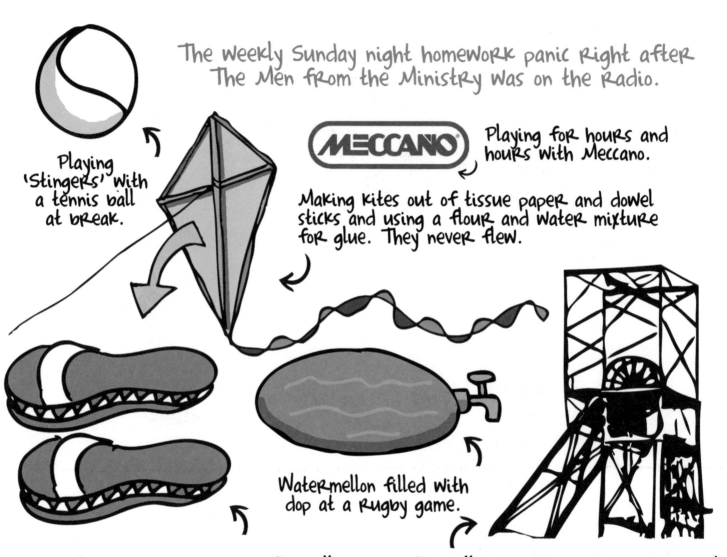

The weekly Sunday night homework panic Right after The Men from the Ministry was on the Radio.

Playing 'Stingers' with a tennis ball at break.

MECCANO

Playing for hours and hours with Meccano.

Making kites out of tissue paper and dowel sticks and using a flour and water mixture for glue. They never flew.

Watermellon filled with dop at a Rugby game.

Sandles made out of old tyres. This is Recycling at it's absolute best!

The Villagers - 'The Village Reef was their home built on a pile of gold'. The Villagers. Ted Dixon, Hilton McCrae, Buller Wilmot and Cheesa Labuschange.

Dinky Toys. →

Reading the Katzenjammer Kids in the Sunday papers and having no clue what the hell was going on.

Created by Dirks and Knerr

Ignore this space.

Collecting Matchbooks.

Some Random soccer club names:

Highlands Park, Lusitano, Jewish Guild, Southern Suburbs, Rangers, Powerlines, Hellenic, Corinthians, Germiston Callies, Dynamos, Durban City, Cape Town City and Arcadia Shepherds.

My parents gave me a moer of a skrik one day when I was a lightie. I was throwing a tantrum or something and would not stop. So they took me to Norwood police station and my old man comes out of the cop shop with a constable and the oke charfs me if I don't behave he's going to gooi me in choekie forever.

Shame man. That wasn't very nice. I still feel sorry for myself hey.

When a teacher said, 'We need to have a LITTLE chit chat,' it actually meant you were in BIG kak.

SHOT CHINA

Using the word 'shot' when saying bye.

BILTONG AND POTROAST

The Biltong and Potroast TV show with Mel Miller, Cyril Green, Eddie Eckstein, Dennis MacLean, Johnny Noble and a bunch of other ous. It was unique for the time and was actually my first intro to stand-up comedy.

Surprise from the general public when Naas Botha played football for the Dallas Cowboys for about five minutes.

The pipe band at high school. Quite stirring really.

When I was on Scholar Patrol. We stopped the St. Andrews Girls school bus every day to say howzit through the windows and the old toppie driver got the moer in with us every day.

'Those were the days my friend. We thought they'd never end. We'd sing and dance forever and a day. We'd live the life we choose. We'd fight and never lose. For we were young and sure to have our way.'

Calling pre-teen facial hair on boys 'bum fluff'.

Reading Lord of the Flies. One of the first books I read for school that I both understood and actually enjoyed.

I was a carrot in the Jabula Park nursery school concert!

Failing maths my whole life and wondering why the hell I needed to do maths for matric when I wanted to write for a living. I'm still wondering.

I was so nervous about failing that I cribbed on my
aptitude test at primary school! The problem was
that the oke I cribbed from was doffer than me.
(Now I know why the teachers spoke to me very
slowly and carefully and enunciated their words.)

Random names I Remember:

Geen and Richards

John Orr's

Deans

Cuthberts

Bothners

Katz and Lurie

Mr. Man

Ackerman's

Stans

Hilton Radio

Mi Vami

FONTANA

bimbo's

pan burgers

BLACK STEER

Turn and Tender

The smiley face.

The smell of sparks and raw electricity at the Dodgem car place on the Esplanade in Durban.

Prestick to put your posters on the wall. It left an oily patch on the poster and on the wall.

Carving a heart on the trunk of a bluegum tree.

Trolls on pencils.

They came with little combs I swear.

Making home-made sherbet with bicarb and icing sugar and it really tasted kaaaaak.

Toasted bacon and banana.

76

Stink bombs from Roys for Toys (and calling a fart a baff).

Saying, 'What a boykie.'

Duwweltjies. (Thorns with two spikes that we often stood on because we were always barefoot.)

My friends Mike Eustace and John Hitchins who died in matric.

Buying plastic things called 45s and LPs from Recordia.

When my favourite cat disappeared and never came back. She was my friend.

RIP.

It was after midnight at a coffee shop on Rocky Street in Yeoville. The street was empty. I could hear my footsteps echoing as I walked. It had just rained and purple and green neon reflected intermittently on the black, wet streets.

As I walked along I could have sworn I heard a wailing saxophone in the distance. But that could have been inside my head. I'm a bit of a romantic.

I noticed you the minute I walked into the coffee shop. Perhaps it was because you were the only one in there. I was surprised that the sound of the door opening didn't make you look up.

You didn't lift your head once while I was drinking my cappuccino. I didn't realise you were weeping until I had finished my coffee. You were clutching a little white tissue and wiping your eyes. I'm sorry I didn't notice your tears when I walked in. I could have consoled you all along. I'm a good listener.

I decided to talk to you. I stood up. I was about to take a step in your direction when he came rushing in. My intention was to rescue you from the depths of your depression. I came up with a perfect opening line that took me about ten minutes to compose. I think I was going to say something extremely profound like, 'Hey, are you okay?'

Too late. He grabbed your arm. I had visions of broken china and splintering tables. He pulled you towards himself so violently I thought he would crack every bone in your body.

I covered my head with my arms and closed my eyes.

I waited for your scream. Nothing. I opened my eyes and saw him sobbing on your shoulder. You kissed his tears and stroked his hair. Then you left in his arms.

I paid for your coffee.

Hello little mouselett.

My brother trying to feed a sweet little white mouse to his pet snake, but instead he saved the mouse and let the snake go. (I think remaining residents of the neighbourhood would still like to know exactly 'where' he let it go.)

When your parents gave you a yucky spoon full of Castor oil to cure a stomach ache. (I actually think it was to cure Bunkalitis.)

Eating flaky pastry sausage rolls from the school tuck shop.

In about standard five, standing on the coffee table with my pants pulled up under my arms singing Mungo Jerry's song 'In The Summertime' and gyrating my hips. (Please don't ask.)

A very old stamp.

This one too.

'The Fabulous Fishheads'. A lekker little television series I devised and presented to the SABC in my second year of the army. They looked at me like I was some kind of Mal Jan from Groendakkies. (I suppose arriving in my browns and wearing a boshoed at an angle on my kop put them off a bit. In retrospect I think laughing my arse off when they asked me if I had seen Haas Das and Bennie Bookwurm was not the best thing to do. What totally shocked me was that they turned me down. Damn fools!

What?

A stance and phrase I often encountered as I was just about to ask a Grove girl (who was way above my low-on-the-totem-pole status) if she wouldn't mind going to movies or playing spin the bottle or something.

The absolute euphoria and total bliss
of being in love for the very first time.

Realising that a cup of tea fixes everything!

The old man who walked around town in the red fez, singing, nee, nee, nee and handing out incense.

Choc 99

Getting my first leather jacket and thinking I was a big breker! (Until the real brekers walked into the party and I just about bloody kakked myself.)

Sweet, innocent love in nursery school.

SATURDAY NIGHT

Watching the Bay City Rollers
at the Coliseum in Jo'burg with
my little sister. (Don't ask.)

Saying goodbye to my toppies at Milner Park and getting on a train to go to basic training. And the painful pretend smiles my parents gave us to try and make us feel better. (My boet and I did our army training together.)

I robbed a bank but I didn't feel guilty because I knew my brother had robbed the same bank the day before when we played Monopoly with the neighbourhood kids. (He taught me some bad stuff my naughty little brother did.)

True confession: As a very little kid I was petrified of the Three Little Pigs.

George MacManus's Bringing up Father.

Jiggs and Maggie.

Distributed by King Features Syndicate.

Getting into kak from my nanny for not taking off my school uniform when I got home and making it dirty. She vloeked me big time and never took any crap!

Take a picture. It will last longer.

Calling boobs, 'numbies'.

Trevor Rabin
Ashley Brokenshaw
Fergie Ferguson
Cindy Alter
Bernie Millar
'Bones' Brettell
Sandy Robbie
Alaister Oakley
Peps Cotumaccio
Gavin Langeveldt
Les Goode
Julian Laxton
Cedric Samson
Freedom's Children
Lancaster Band
McCully Workshop
Clout
Circus
Stingray
Hawk
EllaMental
Ingy Herbst
Morocko
Dog Detachment
Peach
Kettle
Otis Waygood
Backtrax
Sweatband
Suck
PJ Powers
Et al...

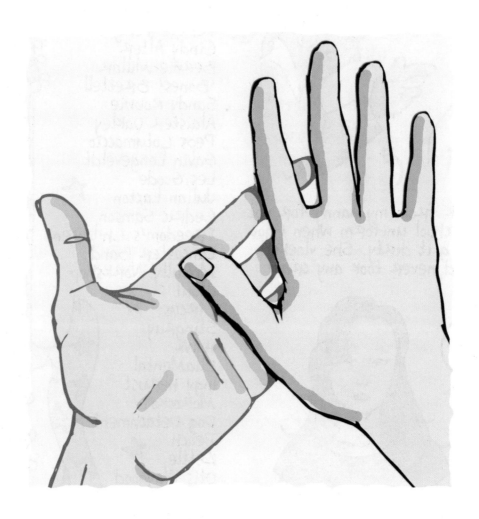

I have a very powerful memory of saying goodbye to my parents at Jan Smuts airport once when I went overseas. In those days they had a thick plate glass divider between the people saying goodbye and the passengers on their way to passport control. You could not hear each other but people gestured and mouthed their goodbyes through the glass before they went into the departures lounge.

It was a hard goodbye for me. I put my hand on the glass and my dad did the same on the other side. We touched our hands together, palm to palm, through the glass. I will never forget that.

Sadly, I was living overseas when my father suddenly died and touching his hand through the glass is how I will always remember saying goodbye to him.

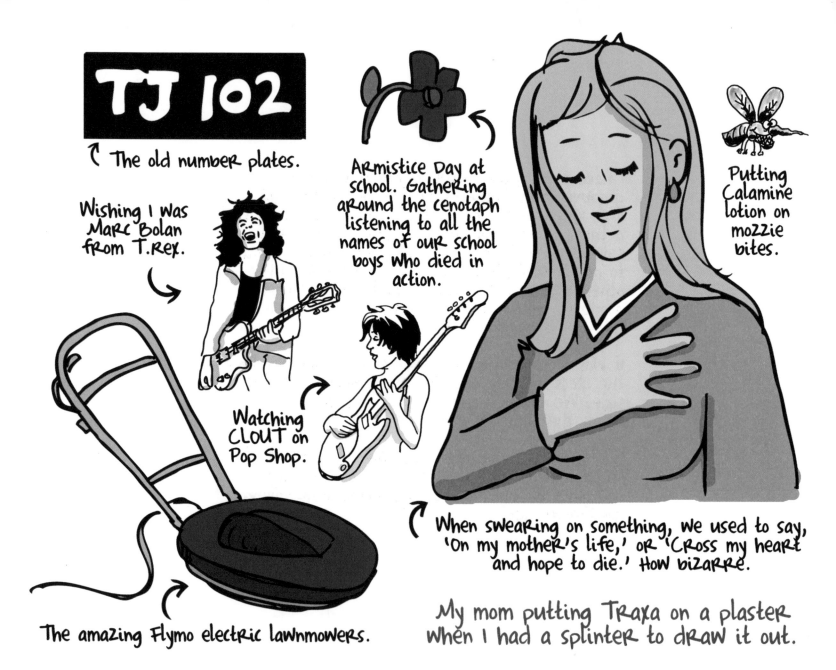

TJ 102

↳ The old number plates.

Wishing I was Marc Bolan from T.Rex.

Armistice Day at school. Gathering around the cenotaph listening to all the names of our school boys who died in action.

Putting Calamine lotion on mozzie bites.

Watching CLOUT on Pop Shop.

The amazing Flymo electric lawnmowers.

When swearing on something, we used to say, 'On my mother's life,' or 'Cross my heart and hope to die.' How bizarre.

My mom putting Traxa on a plaster when I had a splinter to draw it out.

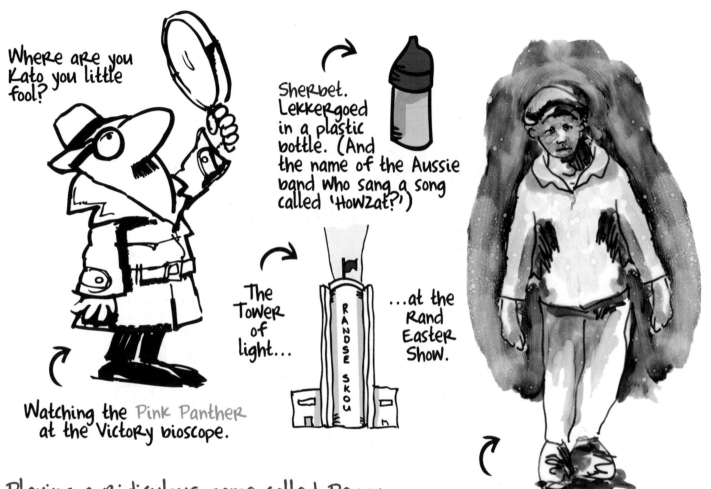

Where are you Kato you little fool?

Watching the Pink Panther at the Victory bioscope.

Sherbet. Lekkergoed in a plastic bottle. (And the name of the Aussie band who sang a song called 'Howzat?')

The Tower of light...

RANDSE SKOU

...at the Rand Easter Show.

Playing a ridiculous game called Peggy. Which entailed throwing a knife or a screwdriver into the ground near someone's foot. And we never ever threw at the person's foot on purpose I swear. (Well...maybe sometimes.)

Stories my late dad told me about his youth. My grandparents struggled financially and my father's father was an angry, violent man. He took a lot of his frustrations out on my dad.

There was always something interesting going on at the corner cafes.

Being busted for stealing sweets from the cafe. It was my first and last major robbery (other than siphoning petrol a few times, stealing food in the army and scaling paper clips & stuff from the office).

'I know you've been smoking and loitering in the cafe with those Italian, Greek, Portuguese, Lebanese and Jewish boys. You are going straight to Maryvale Church, right now, to confess young lady!'

Autograph books at primary school where your friends wrote messages like Roses are red, violets are blue, I am an idiot, and so are you.

Having my tonsils out at the Brenthurst clinic and being upset because the matron wouldn't put them in a jar for me to take home. (I don't think they have matrons anymore.)

When a teacher, who was about to give you cuts, said, 'This is going to hurt me more than it's going to hurt you.' Yeah right!

VRYSTAAT!

When people yelled, 'Vrystaaaat,' for no apparent reason.

Collecting tadpoles in a jar.

Taking a 'shoof' at a chick meant having a 'look'.

Playing gaining ground.

My father listening to Frank Sinatra and singing along with him. (Yikes! I think I hid under my bed when he did.)

The ultimate skaam. My mother dressed my brother and me in the same outfits even though he is two years younger than I am.

Being in love with my mom's friend when I was an early teen. She was fris.

(* I taste you broken.)

I'll never forget trying to translate classic South African phrases for some exchange students from America.

When I was a little oke Sugus put the 'lekker' in lekkergoed for me.

The colourful cabins on Muizenburg beach.

The egg throwing incident. Jirre did we lag. But our grins disappeared bloody quickly when we walked into the door of our house. Joy was short lived because, somehow, my old man had heard all about it before we even got home. (I don't know who the stool pidgeon was but my dad always seemed to hear about our shenanigans.) And yes, I did get a short, sharp, klap upside the head!

Calling our army issue undies Santa Marias after the sail of one of the boats that van Riebeeck arrived on. These did not make women jags.

Hello nurse!

We used the word jags or Jagse Jannie to describe someone (me) who was a tad horny or randy.

X-RAY SPECS

PLASTIC DOG POO

WHOPEE CUSHION

SEA MONKEY

Wishing we could get all the lekker stuff on the back of American comic books that came a year after they were released. Things like X-Ray specs, Sea Monkeys and plastic dog poo.

Padkos

COOLER

BOX

I remember the song, 'She wore an itsy bitsy teenie weenie yellow polka dot bikini.' (I still want to know who she was and where she hung out. It may well have been at Clifton beach.)

Having to swim on chilly mornings at school.

Fipso. Orange juice in a clear plastic bag.

FIPSO

The school girls loved the Jackie magazine filled with pictures of David Cassidy and David Essex.

Jackie

Riding a motorbike (also known as an aut or a boney) for the first time and popping the clutch and landing on my arse as the bike took off and left me in the dust. (Yes of course the word 'skaam' was uttered a lot.) The ous still remind me of it all the time.

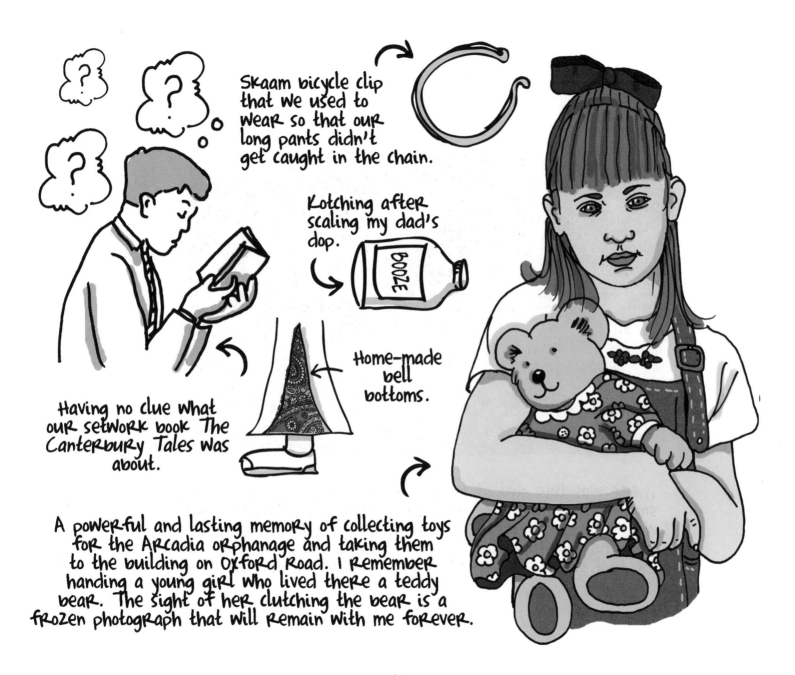

Skaam bicycle clip that we used to wear so that our long pants didn't get caught in the chain.

Kotching after scaling my dad's dop.

BOOZE

Having no clue what our setwork book *The Canterbury Tales* was about.

Home-made bell bottoms.

A powerful and lasting memory of collecting toys for the Arcadia orphanage and taking them to the building on Oxford Road. I remember handing a young girl who lived there a teddy bear. The sight of her clutching the bear is a frozen photograph that will remain with me forever.

There was this girl at the bus stop every day. She always smiled at me. She was beautiful. Each day I planned what I was going to say to her to ask her out, but I was a bang-broek and chickened out. I never spoke to her. I heard years later that she wanted to ask me out but was a bangbroek too.

I once took a dare and got onto a Putco bus. I told the driver about the dare. He played along. I got off at my usual stop. Nobody scowled at me. Nobody robbed me. In fact the riders on the Putco bus didn't give a crap. They just wanted to take their exhausted and weary selves home to Alexandra township.

Maryvale
Early Seventies

First Love

I saw her from across the room. She was bathed in a bright spotlight although there were no spotlights at all in the hall.

To tell the truth there was very little light, except for the neon halo above Jesus' head.

We were at the Maryvale Church Hall. They were having a 'social'. And, for kids from both boys and girls-only schools...

..it was an opportunity to socialize under the watchful eyes of the nuns, the clergy and of course... the Lord Jesus himself.

Girls were dancing in clumps and the boys were ogling at them from the wooden chairs in the hall.

I was sitting with my friends when I saw her.

She was dancing with a group of girls. In my mind she was moving in slow motion.

I stared at her without blinking. I didn't want to take my eyes off her in case she disappeared.

Her friends saw me staring. Hands lifted to mouths in pre-teen giggles. Whispers ensued.

I blushed and dropped my head with embarrassment.

Hey Trev, she's looking at you.

Mark got up and ran.

My friend Mark nudged me urgently. I looked up. To my horror I saw the girl walking toward me.

The chicken.

I wanted to run too, but I froze. The blood suddenly rushed from my feet to my heart, rendering my limbs totally useless. I tried to move but my legs simply refused to respond at all.

Hi. Would you like to

dance?

Huh?

I got up.

Errr okay.

She took my hand.

My knees were jelly.

My mind was toast.

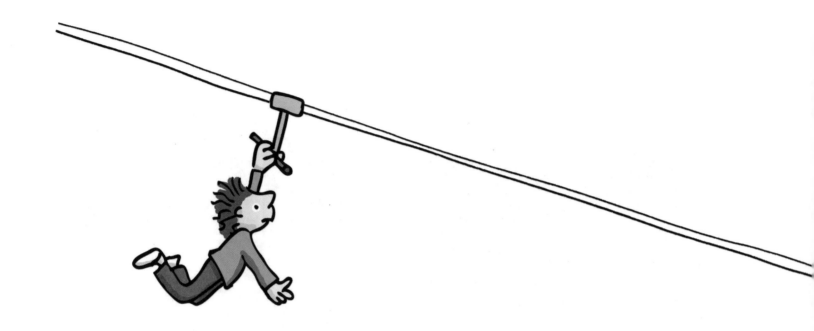

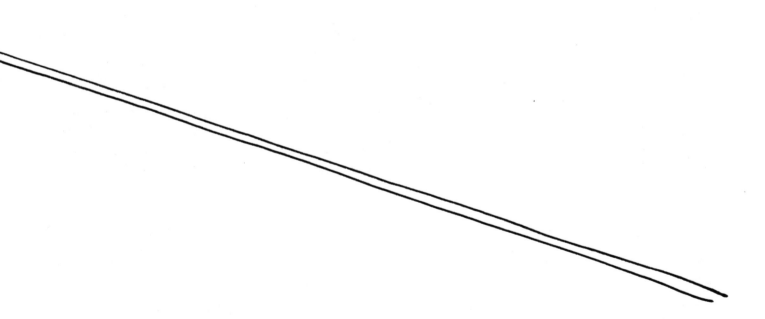

Foefie slides!

The satisfaction of plotting an elaborate scheme to bunk school which actually worked. And then the whole plan being totally buggered up when the headmaster walked into the cafe where we were playing pinball. (I dug myself into a deeper hole when I pointed out that, in essence, he was bunking too. Not well-received mind you.)

When you had a bad cough, your mom would make you put a towel over your head and force you to inhale steam from a bowl of boiling water and that stuff called FRiaRS Balsam.

Hot WateR Bottles in winter. (Often with a knitted jersey to stop you from burning the bloody crap out of your feet.)

Kids putting chalk under their tongues at primary school because apparently you would faint and be sent home. It didn't work and it tasted kak.

Playing noughts and crosses with wet fingers on the slasto next to a pool.

Going for a drive on Sundays.

remember that first real kiss when you were a jags teenager?

Falling asleep, during a moer of a Transvaal storm, feeling safe and sound.

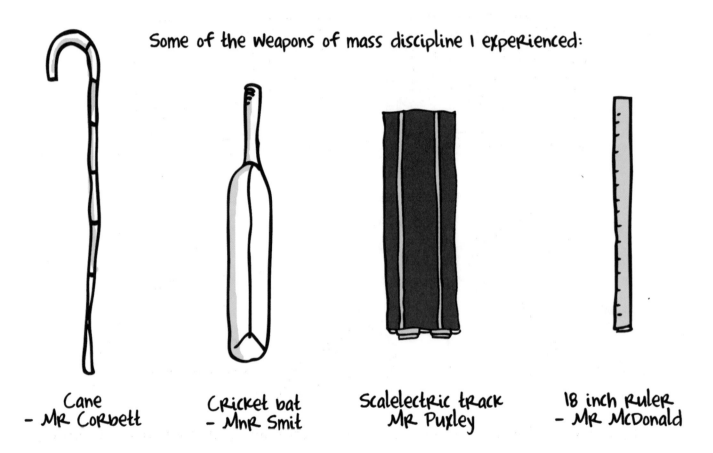

Transvaal Education Department's official
Tools of ~~Torture~~ Discipline

Some of the weapons of mass discipline I experienced:

Cane
– Mr Corbett

Cricket bat
– Mnr Smit

Scalelectric track
Mr Puxley

18 inch ruler
– Mr McDonald

Dual-airflow
aerated paddle
- Mr Wilson

Totally gnawed, dog-breath-saturated,
sat, old swing-ball on a string
- Mrs Du Plessis

size extra-large
takkie
- Mr McFarland

Cortina 3 litre
Escourt fan belt.
- Mr Harrison

EINA!

Totally buggered
up ping pong bat
- Mev. Schoeman

Genuine Eastern Transvaal hand-picked
and personally whittled willow
- Mr Nel

On a school trip to Swaziland I left my wallet (which my grandpa gave me) in a souvenir shop. A little boy with beads in his hair chased after the bus and gave my wallet back. Nothing was missing.

Waking up to the smell of coffee in the bush. The wonderful
feeling of lying in my sleeping bag and listening to the
amazing sounds of dawn's insect symphony. Slowly realising,
for the first time, that Africa will always be a part of me.

Green Mielieeeees.   Sugar caaaane. Mielieeeees. (Sharp wistle) Mielieeees. Sugar caaaane.

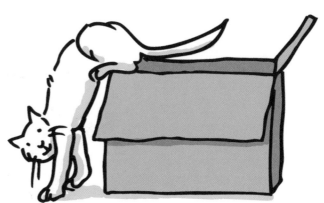

← My childhood cat Tai Tai.

Being petrified of my aunty Mushie's boobs. Especially during the vast, all-enveloping, perfume-overloaded hugs in which the words 'total asphyxiation' come to mind.

Mielieeeees. (Sharp wistle) Mielieeees. Sugar caaaane. Mielieeeees. (Sharp whistle)

Bus conductor's (Klippie's) coin and ticket machine.

'Ohhh Je' Taime' Jane Birkin

My inner child

love is...

The, err, slightly corny Love Is cartoons by Kim Casali were a big hit in Std Five.

The sadness of going back to your army base on a Sunday night after your first weekend pass and leaving family and the stukkie at the station. That was kak man!

121

My late dad's warm, wonderful, amazing, smile.
He was such a lekker oke I swear!

Listening to horse racing on the radio. Muis Roberts racing
at Turfontein. Also Marty Schoeman and his filly.

Vague memories of sitting in my dad's MORRIS MINOR.

Boxes were much better to play with than toys.

Des and Dawn's **GODSPELL**

Blue bottles. Eina!

Being deeply moved when hearing a young nanny up the Road with a beautiful voice singing Thula Thula Baba! It still gives me goosies.

Writing lines for punishment!

I will not write on walls ever again.
I will not write on walls ever again.
I will not write on walls ever again.
I will not write on walls

Playing touch rugby with the neighbourhood kids almost every day after school.

Proudly watching my childhood friend Chesney play number eight for Transvaal schools and then for Transvaal.

In the Sunday newspaper.

Making a home-made skateboard with rollerskate wheels and an old plank.

Canoeing down the Vaal River from the Barrage to Parys, with my buddy Mark, and almost kakking myself when a giant likkewaan scrambled over the boat as we were climbing some rocks to get past a weir on the water.

125

The men working on the roads. An unchained chain gang. Doing the work of a bulldozer with ungloved hands and pick axes. Singing hauntingly beautiful harmonies followed by deep resonating grunts and the sound of the picks hitting the ground as one.

Beautiful music swirling around the flying dust and grit. A sight that is, thankfully, long gone but the stirring a cappella voices still echo in my mind.

When I was a little boy my dad told the BEST stories. I would stand behind him in the car with my arms around him as we drove to Vredefort where my grandparents lived. He once told me the most fascinating story about a little boy who found a star. I think I drove my old man nuts because I begged for that story every time we got into the car. I swear he must have told it to me a thousand times.

Writing my own absent note after bunking school and actually believing I'd get away with it.

My first love letter.

Climbing up and down mine dumps without getting cyanide poisoning.

GOLD

Pipe cleaners

Hey man, why am I so damn hungry?

Being bored out of my skull on Sunday afternoons before TV when my parents went for a kip and all that was left to do was to listen to Esmé Everard on the radio.

Peeling Bostik off my fingers.

Being one of the only okes in the world I know who didn't smoke zol but got klank gerook from all the ous skyfing in the car.

132

Mr Paul Climgan. An amazing teacher who inspired me the most. He got the creativity in my brain all stirred up. He allowed me to write song lyrics for an essay. He would bring his guitar into class and sing to his students. I never bunked his class once. He taught me my favourite Winnie the Pooh saying.

'DON'T UNDERESTIMATE THE VALUE OF DOING NOTHING, OF JUST SITTING AND LISTENING TO ALL THE THINGS YOU CAN'T HEAR.'

— WINNIE THE POOH

The old HB pencil. Great to draw with. Perfect sharp point to poke the person's neck sitting in front of you in class.

'These boots were made for walking and that's just what they'll do. One of these days these boots gonna walk all over you.'

You never forget the first time.

I still remember it to this day. My dad was the one who drove me to Hillbrow and doubled-parked the car while I went inside. My dad was a cool oke. Often the instigator of shenanigans. He was with me all the way on this one.

Because it was the first time for me, I must admit, I was rather nervous. It didn't take long. Actually a bit too quickly for my liking. Somewhat of a letdown considering how pumped I was for that first experience.

And, the best part of it was that I used my own money!

The transaction was a blur to tell the truth. I don't remember much of what happened when money passed hands.

Totally satisfied though, I walked out of the shop door, smiling like a Cheshire cat. In my hands I clutched a seven single, otherwise known as a forty-five, of Otis Redding's 'Dock of the Bay'. I turned and looked back at the store.

I smiled to myself.

Mission accomplished.

I had bought my very first record. And then we went for coffee.

You never forget the first time.

135

The danger of playing tok-tokkie. Especially if the oke came after you with a sjambok or a knopkierie. Jirre!

Playing the Cold Fact album by Rodriguez while I was graunching, which is a forgotten word for heavy petting.

doll house

COKE ADDS LIFE
HAMBURGERS
HOT DOGS
DURBAN POISON

BIG FIGHT SAT NIGHT
YEOVILLE OKES VS
GROVE OKES. HERE

SHAKES
APPLE PIE
OBEX

COKE ADDS LIFE

doll house

The Doll House. Where many a fight, romance, friendship, boerie roll, jol, banana milkshake, motorbike race and other kak happened almost every weekend.

DOLL HOUSE

Calling a toilet 'the bogs'. And calling toilet paper 'bogroll'.

Nothing better than a toasted sarmie as a pre-hangover meal on a saturday night.

136

Standing beat during my basic training and feeling so lonely. Although they were breaking us down, and building us up to be rough and tough and ready, the little boy who was still inside me was totally bewildered and scared.

Duh. Making blood brothers with my actual brother who was already a blood relative because we had the same toppies.

(The incident included my famous last words. 'Ag man it won't hurt. Grandpa's pocket knife is really bloody sharp hey.')

Guy Fawkes day. The burning of a 'guy' in a wheel barrow, or in a box or an old bath tub. Think about it. We cheered and danced around a burning guy. An oke on fire, ek sê!

Hitching was the way we got around in the olden days.

Sometimes you'd get picked up by an oke in a bakkie that was so dronk he'd jam on brakes and we'd all going flying to the front of the bakkie, then he'd accelerate and we'd almost fall off the back. And you'd be banging on the top of the cab for him to stop. And he would stop, like ten blocks after you wanted to get off. Then he'd reverse back up the road at 90 miles an hour into on-coming traffic.

Then you'd get the oke driving an old Zephyr who was so gerook that he would drive at 10 kilometres an hour and think he was driving 120. His eyes bigger and redder than the blerrie brake lights of the jammy in front of him.

You sometimes get involved in a domestic dispute between a couple sitting as far away from each other in the front seat of their Cortina 3 litre Escourt as possible. And you were the go-between.

'Tell him I'm not going to Plum Crazy. Skollies go there.'

'She said I must tell you ...'

'Yes, I heard what she said, she's sitting right next to me. Tell her I'm not going to Raffles with the larny's. I am going to Plum Crazy to listen to Circus.'

'He said he's not...'

'Yes I heard what he #$♡@ said. Tell him I want to hear Julian Laxton not that kak pop music.'

Ja hitching. Too dangerous now but what a joll it was.

138

In such a loud voice so everyone in the whole friggin' posie could hear.

PLAIN OR RIBBED?

From behind my hand (that was hiding a giant zit) I asked the pharmacist for chorb cream at the Daelite pharmacy in Orange Grove and somehow the oke thought I was asking for a condom.

Aaaiieee. I'm still cringing!

Phoning random numbers and asking if people's fridge was running. And if they said yes telling them to run after it.

Jody Scheckter our very own World Champion racing at Kyalami.

EINA!

A bit of toothpaste in your eye mimicked pink eye. A great way to bunk school.

My dad teaching me how to shave.

My nanny sprouting an avocado with tooth picks in a glass of water on the kitchen windowsill

Personality, Scope, You and Huisgenoot magazines full of important skandaal, gossip and pictures of popular South African celebrities with stories about Glenda Kemp's python and ou Charlie Weir's hair. These periodicals were a perfect fit in the back of your rods when you were about to get cuts at school.

PERSONALITY
SONJA HERHOLDT

Piet. The sweet, gentle toppie who managed my grandpa's farm. He was such a great guy. So calm and quietly strong. In a different era he may well have been a sage or an elder or even run an orphanage. I made him a pipe out of a mielie cob when I was about eight or nine. He thanked me profusely and smiled broadly when I gave it to him. He smoked it every time I went to visit the farm. I wish he was still around. He'd make a wonderful mentor.

Catching a fat skaam at primary school. Getting caught passing a love letter.

Biting the edges of our beds when we were in the army to make sure they were perfectly square. Then we'd sleep on the floor so the beds would not get messed up. Strue's God.

Wearing a cardboard box as armour in grade one playing the role of Don Quixote in a play without having a clue who he was or what the story was about. (Still don't.)

Wanting to hide every time people sang, 'For he's a jolly good fellow'.

My dentist's name was Dr Hammer. (I swear.)

'Your teeth are vrot my boy. This won't hurt a bit I promise.'

Liar liar pants on fire!

Typical Vaalie! Sunburn on your back on the very first day of holidays at the beach.

And he wasn't skaam to use those pliers.

Sometimes the paper stuck to the ice cream and it was hard to get off. Sometimes it even stuck to your damn lip or tongue!

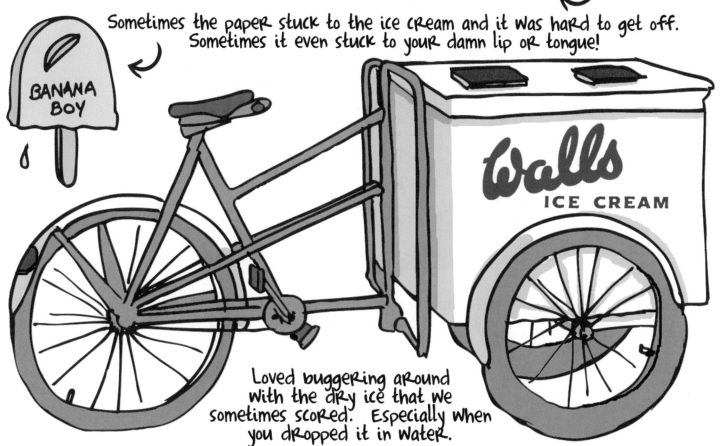

Loved buggering around with the dry ice that we sometimes scored. Especially when you dropped it in water.

Following the Cape to Rio yacht race on a chart.
(Every day they had co-ordinates on the radio.)

Me and my boet going to Durban by train on our aces.
(At ten and eleven years old.)

'Goeie genade! There's blerrie ball hairs in your @#+% rifle, Romain.' – Bdr PvS (Name witheld because I'm still kak scared of the oke.)

Eskimo Pie. This was my best ice cream of all time!

Walls

Playing Smoke on the Water a million times.

Braai in a wheelbarrow.

Ticky the Clown (and Sixpence) from the Boswell-Wilkie Circus.

Watching the groot bek bully at our primary school crying after he chirped one of the girls in our class and she klapped him across the face. Jeez did we all catch a lag that day. (Not in front of him.)

Lecol. Sometimes known as lethal due to Orange Dye #56532b which closed your throat and almost histamined you to death.

Lecol

The cowboy skop, skiet en donder movies (also known as spaghetti westerns) including, 'The Good, the Bad and the Ugly', 'A Fist Full of Dollars', 'They call me Trinity' and, 'God forgives...I Don't' with Terence Hill and Bud Spencer.

The klippie got the moer in when kids rang the bell twice for the bus to go, then they jumped off, and the bus started moving before eveyone was off. The klippie would yell at the ous as they ran away. One time my friend Ronnie jumped (or was pushed) off the bus and he ran smack bang into the open door of the Atlas bread van that was double parked outside Thelma's Cafe. Eina!

HIGHLANDS

13 CITY/STAD

TJ 1015

AAAAAAAAAAAHHHHHHHHH HHHHHHHH

Over a cup of Five Roses tea just before my Matric exams my dad asked me what I thought was the most important thing I learned at school. This is what I told him. (Actually I didn't learn it at school. I really learned it from hearing it many times at assembly BEFORE school.) I still remember it to this very day...

Start here.

Lord, make me an instrument of your peace.

Where there is hatred, let me sow love.

Where there is injury, pardon. Where there is doubt, faith.

Where there is despair, hope.
Where there is darkness, light.
Where there is sadness, joy.

Grant that I may not so much seek to be consoled, as to console.

To be understood, as to understand; to be loved, as to love.

For it is in giving that we receive.
It is in pardoning that we are pardoned.

– Saint Francis of Assisi

WARNING!

Don't grow up.
It's a trap!

And now, if you'll excuse me,
I'm off to start a new chapter...

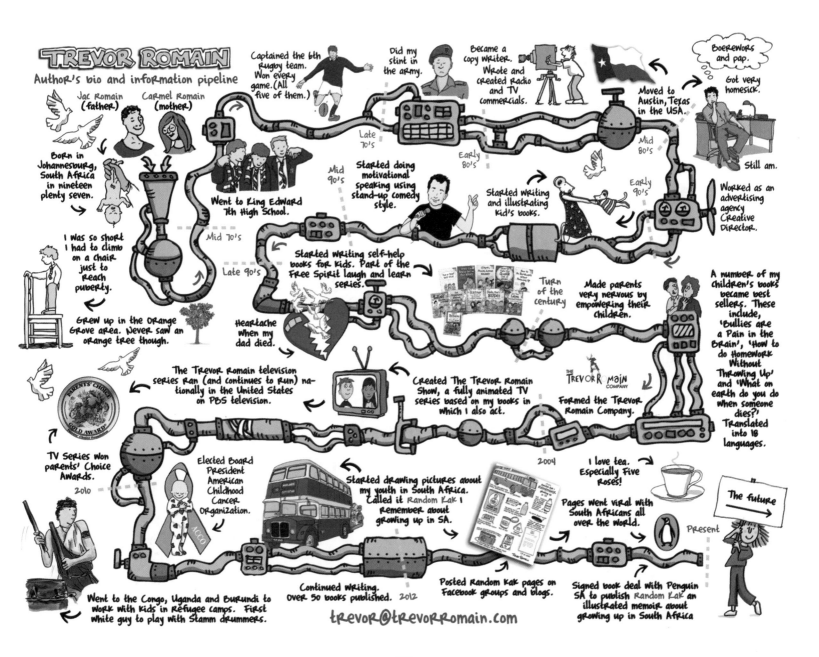

GLOSSARY

Ace	Alone
Ag	Oh. Often indicating irritation or exasperation
Bang-broek	Fraidy cat
Boerie roll	Boerewors (sausage) on a bun
Boet	Brother
Bollemakiesie	Somersault, head over heels
Boshoed	Bush hat worn by soldiers while in the bush
Breker	Tough guy
Buggered off	Disappeared. Went away
Charf	Chat up
Chirp	Speak to (someone) in a taunting way
Choekie	Prison
Chorb	Pimple
Coming short	Having a mishap
Cuts	Caned, corporal punishment at school
Diep kak	Deep shit
Dof	Dim. Not smart
Drommies	Drum majorettes
Dronk	Drunk
Eina	Ouch
Fris	Powerful and strong
Gat	Arse, backside
Gerook	Stoned
Gooi	Throw
Goosies	Goose bumps
Grils	The chills. Goose bumps
Groot bek	Big mouth
Howzit?	Hello. How is it going?
Jirre	Oh my God
Joll	To party and have fun
Kak	Crap/shit
Klap	Smack/slap
Klaring out	Getting out of the army
Klippie	Bus conductor
Kop	Head
Kotch (English)	Vomit
Kots (Afrikaans)	Vomit
Laaitie	A youngster. Also spelled lightie
Lag/lagging	Laugh/laughing
Lamer	To punch someone in the bicep muscle or to use a knee to hit someone in the thigh. This causes lameness
Lekker	Nice
Lightie	A youngster. Also spelled laaitie
Ma	Mother
Mampoer	Homemade liquor, moonshine
Mielie	Corn
Min dae	Not many days left (often related to the end of National Service)
Moer	Beat up. Also an expletive of rage
Mozzie	Mosquito
My china	My mate
Naaier	F*#@er
Nineteen-voetsek	Way back in the nineteen-somethings
Nooit	No way
Oke	A guy
Old ballies	Old folks
Ou	Guy
Ousie	Sister. (Respectful term for domestic worker or nanny)
Pip	Head
Piss cat	Drunkard
Poep scared	Scared shitless
Schloep	Teacher's pet. Goody-two-shoes
Se moer	Your mother
Sies	Yuk/Gross. An exclamation of disgust
Shongololo	A type of millipede that rolls itself into a circle for protection if touched
Skaam	Embarrassment
Skollie	A street hoodlum
Skop, skiet and donder	Kick, shoot and beat up. Usually to describe cowboy movies
Skyf	Smoke
Slap chips	Sloppy French fries
Smaak you stukkend	Love you to pieces
Snuff	A fine-ground tobacco, intended for use by being sniffed into the nose (don't ask me why)
Stop tuning me grief	Stop giving me a hard time
Strue's God	As true as God
Stukkie	A girl
The moer in	Fed up
Tokoloshe	To the superstitious, an evil spirit that can take on various forms. Believed to be short and troll-like
Tok-tokkie	The kids' game of knocking on someone's door and running away
Toppies	Old people
Tweetalig	Bilingual
Vaalie	Someone who came from the Transvaal Province, now Gauteng
Voetsek	Go away (usually to a dog)
Vloek	Swear
Vrot	Rotten
Woes	Angry
You are stripping my moer, bliksem	You're getting on my nerves, bastard
Zol	Marijuana